For
Pam and Alice
Chris and Deenie
Mark and Diana
and Lloyd

This book, especially designed for young children, is a brief retelling of the first part of a famous book entitled *The Black Stallion* and originally published by Random House of New York in 1941.

When the children are a little older, they will want to read the whole story, many times longer than this, just as it was written by Walter Farley.

3 1969 01926 8076

Copyright © 1941, 1953 by Walter Farley
Copyright renewed 1981 by Walter Farley and Random House, Inc.

All rights reserved. Published in the United States by Random House Children's Books, a division of Random House, Inc., New York.

RANDOM HOUSE and colophon are registered trademarks of Random House, Inc.

www.randomhouse.com/kids

Educators and librarians, for a variety of teaching tools, visit us at www.randomhouse.com/teachers

Library of Congress Control Number: 53-6288

ISBN: 978-0-375-84035-7 (trade) — ISBN: 978-0-375-94054-5 (lib. bdg.)

MANUFACTURED IN MALAYSIA   10 9 8 7 6 5 4 3 2 1

BIG BLACK HORSE

Adapted from *The Black Stallion* by

Walter Farley

illustrated by James Schucker

1. The Black

In a country far across the sea lived a big black horse. He had a long tail, a long mane, and long legs. His head was small, and so were his ears, but his eyes were large and bright. He had always run wild and free. He had no name—he was just called the Black.

One day some men caught him, blindfolded him, and tried to put him on a ship. They pulled him hard with long ropes and hit him with whips. The Black became very angry. He rose high on his hind legs and pawed the air. Then he screamed and plunged forward, hitting one of the men with his hooves. The man fell to the ground and lay still. For a long while the big black horse fought hard, but at last the men held him and managed to get him onto the ship. He was pulled into a small stall and tied. Then the door was firmly shut and bolted, and the ship steamed away.

On the deck of that ship, red-haired Alec Ramsay was
standing alone. His parents had sent him to visit his uncle in
India, and now he was on his way home and back to school.

Alec had watched the fight between the men and the horse, and he felt very sorry for the big Black. The boy loved horses, and always got along well with them. Never in his life had he used a whip on a horse.

Day after day, as they sailed the sea, Alec listened to the Black trying to break out of his stall. He heard the strong hooves crashing against its wooden sides. The Black was the wildest horse he had ever seen!

One night Alec went to the horse's stall, carrying in his hand some lumps of sugar. It was so dark inside the stall he couldn't see the horse. He could hear him, though! So Alec talked to the Black. He told him that he was his friend and that he would never harm him. After a long while Alec left the lumps of sugar on top of the stall door and went to his cabin. Later, when he returned, the sugar was gone.

Every night after that, Alec would go to the Black's stall, leave the sugar, and go away. Sometimes he would see the Black, but at other times he would only hear the angry ring of hooves against the floor.

One evening the air was hot and still. Heavy clouds blacked out the stars, and long streaks of lightning raced through the sky. When Alec went to the stall, the Black had his head over the door. He was looking out to sea, and his nostrils were sniffing the air. He turned, whistled when he saw Alec, then looked out to sea again.

Alec was very happy. It was the first time the Black hadn't drawn back into the stall at sight of him. He moved closer and put out some sugar. The Black looked at it, then at the boy. Slowly he moved nearer and began to eat the sugar. Alec watched him for a moment, knowing that the horse was beginning to trust him. Then he went back to his cabin.

2. The Storm

Alec was awakened very suddenly in the middle of the night. A terrible storm had arisen, and Alec was thrown out of bed by the rolling of the ship. There were loud crashes of thunder, followed by flashes of lightning that made the cabin as bright as day.

With trembling hands, Alec hastily pulled on his clothes. Then he reached under his bunk for a life jacket, fastened it around him, and opened the door. Out in the passageway, people were shouting and running. Suddenly there was a crash louder than any of the others.

The ship shook. Alec heard someone shout, "She's been struck! We're sinking. The ship is going down!"

Alec ran up on deck and, looking about, saw people scrambling into lifeboats. As Alec waited his turn to get into a boat, he suddenly thought of the big black horse. What was happening to him? Was he still in his stall? He must be given a chance to be saved, too!

Fighting his way out of the crowd huddled at the rail, Alec
ran toward the stern of the ship.

He could hear the Black snorting and neighing. Alec
opened the stall door and the horse came rushing out, for he

had broken the rope that held him. The boy tried to get out of his way, but too late! As the big black horse plunged for an opening in the rail, he hit Alec's shoulder, knocking the boy into the sea with him. Alec felt the water close over his head.

Alec's life jacket brought him quickly to the surface again. As he turned to swim back to the ship, an explosion shook the air, and he saw that the ship was sinking rapidly. Frantically he looked around for a lifeboat, but there was none to be seen. Then suddenly he saw the Black, swimming close by. The broken rope still hung from the horse's halter. Without stopping to think, Alec grabbed hold of it. In another moment he was being pulled through the stormy sea!

All night long the Black swam, pulling Alec behind him. The boy was very, very tired and weak from battling the high waves, but the big horse kept on swimming steadily.

When morning came, the storm had ended and the sea was quiet. Alec raised his head and looked about him. There, in the distance, was a white sandy beach!

Faster and faster swam the Black, and soon he was on the beach, pulling Alec right up on the sand.

Alec let go of the rope and lay still, exhausted. The big black horse had saved him from drowning!

3. The Island

Alec slept for a long while. When he awoke, he felt much better, but he was very thirsty. In the sand he saw the hoof prints of the big horse. Alec got up and followed them, for he knew that the horse would find fresh water, if any was to be found.

He crossed the beach and climbed a hill. From where he stood, he could see all around. He was on a small island, mostly sandy and with only a few trees, bushes, and patches of grass showing.

Still following the Black's hoof prints, he went on until he came to a small pool of fresh water. And there was the Black beside it! The wild horse whistled and pawed furiously at the earth when he saw the boy, but made no move to harm him.

So Alec threw himself down on the ground, plunged his face into the cool, clear water, and drank and drank until he had had enough. Then he fell into a deep sleep again.

When he awoke the next morning, he was terribly hungry, but he had to be satisfied with some berries.

Now to make some shelter for himself. He went to the beach and picked up some driftwood. With this he built a small shed.

As he lay down to rest, he saw the Black moving about from one place to another, looking for small patches of grass. "He's as hungry as I am," thought Alec as he closed his eyes.

The next morning Alec made his way toward the rocky side of the island. There he found a lot of sea moss growing on the rocks at the water's edge. He pulled off whole handfuls of the moss and hurried back to the spring with it. There he washed it carefully in the fresh water to take away the salty flavor of the sea, and set it out in the sun to dry.

After a little while Alec tasted it. It wasn't bad. He ate some more, and left the rest on the ground beside the pool. Would the Black eat it, too? Alec hurried to his shelter and watched anxiously. Soon the horse rushed up, shook his head, and took a long drink of water. Next he put his nose to the ground and walked over toward the moss. He sniffed it at first, then tasted a little of it. Then he ate it all.

That night Alec slept better than at any time since he had been on the island. He had found food for his horse and for himself.

From that day on, the big black horse knew that Alec was his friend. He was still a very wild horse. But the boy was kind to him, so the Black never snorted or kicked or showed his teeth when Alec came near him. At last something more wonderful happened. One day the Black let Alec climb upon his back and ride him.

Every day after that, Alec rode the Black up and down the beach. Sometimes the horse would rear when Alec tried to mount him, but the boy would speak softly in his ear, and then the Black would quiet down.

Alec grew to love the Black and to wonder how he would get him home. He wanted to ride him in the park and show him to his friends. But how would either of them ever get off this island?

They had been on it for nineteen days, and the weather was turning cold.

That night Alec put more wood on the fire he had been able to start to keep him warm. Then he crawled wearily into his shelter. Soon he was fast asleep.

He didn't know how long he had been sleeping when the Black's shrill scream awakened him. The top of his shed was on fire! Alec leaped to his feet and rushed outside. A strong wind was blowing, and instantly he saw what had happened. Sparks from his campfire had been blown upon the top of the shelter and had set fire to the dry wood.

The fire burned until early dawn, and when it was over, Alec's shelter was gone. There was nothing for him to do but try to build a new one. The Black trotted ahead of him as he went toward the beach to look for some wood.

At the crest of the hill, Alec suddenly stopped. There below him was a ship anchored a few hundred yards off the island!

4. The Rescue

Alec heard voices. Looking down, he saw a boat being drawn up on the beach by five men.

"You were right, Pat, there *is* someone on this island!" he heard one of the men shout. And another man said, "Sure, and I knew I saw the light of a big fire burning here last night!"

Alec shouted for joy. "We're going home, Black!" he yelled
to his horse. "We're going home!"

The sailors couldn't believe their eyes when they saw Alec, for he was a strange sight. His red hair was overgrown and tangled, and his thin body, browned by the sun, was covered with only a few shreds of clothing. When Alec told the sailors how he had been pulled through the stormy sea by a big black horse, they thought he must be imagining things. But when he called the Black, and the fiery horse came running down the hill to him, the sailors could no longer doubt his word.

They stepped back in their fear of the Black, and watched with wonder in their eyes when Alec patted and coaxed the big black horse toward them. Then Alec said, "You'll take him, too, won't you? I can't leave him behind!"

"He's too wild. We couldn't take him. We couldn't handle him!" came the captain's answer.

"But *I* can handle him," Alec pleaded. The Black was still, his head turned toward the ship as if he understood what was going on. "Please," Alec said. "He saved my life. I can't leave him here alone. He'll die!"

"But how are you going to get him out there?" the captain asked, pointing to the anchored ship.

"He can swim," Alec answered eagerly. "He'll follow me. I know he will."

The captain talked to his men about it and then said, "All right, son—you win. Now let's see you get him to the ship."

"Come on, Black," Alec said, standing up in the boat while the sailors began rowing slowly. "Come on, Black!" he urged, raising his voice. "Swim, Black! Swim!"